The Land of The Eighteen

Kingdoms

by

David Powell

(Illustrations by Stewart Houghton)

For my family:

With love from Pops x

Not long ago, in a land not far from here,

King Even was woken from his sleep by a

loud scream. He sat in the darkness as laughter echoed

around his room.

'Who's there?' asked the King as he leaped from his

bed.

'Come quickly, Sire!' one of the palace guards shouted.

'The Green Witch has kidnapped Princess Faithful!'

King Even ran to his daughter's bedroom and sank to

his knees as he read a note that had been pinned to her

bed -

BY THE TIME YOU HAVE READ THIS IT
WILL BE TOO LATE, YOU FOOL!
THE PRINCESS IS TO MARRY MY SON,
GRIM AND NOTHING YOU CAN DO
WILL STOP IT!
THE WEDDING WILL BE IN TEN DAYS -
YOU MAY EVEN GET AN INVITE.

THE GREEN WITCH

That morning, the king summoned his council to the Great Hall.

'What am I to do, my people?' he asked. 'The Green Witch has kidnapped Princess Faithful and has imprisoned her in the Thirteenth Castle.'

The king was the ruler of the nine Even Lands of the Great Fairway Kingdom. He was dearly loved by all of his subjects but in between the Even Lands were the Odd Lands which were inhabited by nasty troll like creatures called Grumblies. Covered in long black hair, they roamed the Odd Lands, mainly at night with their leader, an awesome looking Grumbly called Grubb.

He was feared by all of the Grumblies and served only the Green Witch.

Grubb

The Green Witch hated King Even and all of his sub-

jects. She dearly wished to rule over all of his nine kingdoms so planned to have the princess marry her son, Grim, to force the king into a pact that would ensure she became overall ruler of the Great Fairway kingdom.

King Even sighed as he looked down at Princess Faithful's pet dog, Sheahan. He spoke to his council-

'Bring me the champions of all the Even Kingdoms. They are my only hope of saving the princess.'

One by one the champions made their way to the palace, travelling day and night past the perilous Odd Hole kingdoms, hoping not to be seen by Grubb's troll army. Little did they know that the prying eyes of the Grumblies were all around them.

Within four days the weary travellers had arrived and nine champions sat before the King in the Great Hall.

'Time is not on our side, my Champions,' the worried King said. 'You have but six days to reach the Thirteenth Castle and rescue the princess. I wish I could tell you how, but all I can ask is that you try. My son, Prince Aydo, will accompany you in this our time of need.'

The King and his council retired from the great hall. Prince Aydo turned and looked toward the tired band of hero's.

'Thank you for coming to our aid. You know who I am, so now please introduce yourselves.' The first of the champions stepped forward.

'I am Skudo, Sire.' The tall, thin young man bowed as he spoke. 'I am the champion pole climber of the Second Kingdom.' Skudo stepped back as the second of the group stood up.

'Pojo's my name, Sire. I am champion of the Fourth Kingdom and I can talk to the creatures of the forest.' He returned to his seat as another stepped forward.

'My name is Dando. I am champion strongman of the Sixth Kingdom and I would dearly love something to eat after the long journey here.' The prince laughed and asked for food and drink to be brought in. He then turned his attention to the next member of the group.

'Now you, little man. What's your name?'

'Chippo is my name, Sire, and I'm the champion acrobat from the Eighth Kingdom.' He gestured toward another of the group. 'This here is my friend Zippo. He's the fastest runner and champion of the Tenth Kingdom. Zippo bowed and then sprinted around the hall at such speed he disappeared from view.

'Where has he gone!?' the surprised prince asked.

'Don't worry your Highness. I am Tracer, champion tracker of the Twelfth Kingdom. 'I can always find him.'

The prince was almost knocked to the floor by the rush of wind as Zippo returned to the group. A strong hand reached out and caught the prince's arm, then helped to dust him off.

'I am Picco, Sire, and I am the champion boxer of the Fourteenth Kingdom.'

'Thank you, Picco,' the prince smiled. 'Zippo really is very fast!'

The last of the champions were Laima and Leema, two sisters from the Sixteenth and Eighteenth Kingdoms who were able to communicate with each other by thought.

When all the introductions had been completed the prince and his champions talked into the early hours.

'We will need to travel by day and night if we are to reach the princess in time,' Skudo said wearily.

'Yes,' said Chippo. 'We will also have to avoid the giants that roam the fair-lands by day and the great white boulders that fall from the sky.'

'But how are we to rescue the princess?' Pojo said. 'She will be heavily guarded by Grumblies. Before we reach the Thirteenth Castle, we have to cross the Flowing River, then the Great Black Divide. That has never been done by day because of the giants.'

'Enough of this worrying!' said Tracer. 'We must leave soon or we will never save the princess!'

'I have heard of a wise old tree that the animals of the forest often speak of,' Pojo said. 'Perhaps if I speak to them, they will take us to it. It might help with our quest.'

'Then let us make haste,' the prince said. 'For we have no time to waste.'

Zippo wasted no time and quickly ran to the edge of the Eighteenth Kingdom to keep a lookout for grumblies, but by now the morning sun was beginning to rise and soon the giants would be walking the fair-lands.

Meanwhile Pojo called to his friends, the squirrels, and asked if they knew of a great wise tree but all they could tell him was that it was near the dreaded Thirteenth Kingdom.

In a flash, Zippo arrived back with the others.

'Hurry!' he said. Time to move - the Grumblies are going to ground to avoid the giants!'

'We must cut around the edge of Willow Wood,' Tracer said. 'That will be the safest way past the giants and their white rocks.'

**

The journey was difficult and the daylight had almost gone as the brave band of champions made their way to the flatlands of the Sixteenth Kingdom.

'Look out!' shouted Chippo as a great white boulder landed inches away from them.

'Giants!' Quickly! Head for the woods,' Dando ordered. The champions hid amongst the massive roots of the trees as they waited for the giants to pass. When the way was clear, they approached the entrance to the

Sixteenth Kingdom. Skudo proceeded to climb down the flagpole and triggered a secret lever known only to the Even people. Suddenly a loud clunking noise could be heard as wooden gears started to turn, opening the cover of the secret entrance just enough for the champions to climb in before it slammed shut behind them.

'Has anyone got any food?' Dando pleaded, having already eaten all the supplies he'd set off with.

'Do you ever stop eating, Dando?' Prince Aydo laughed. The champions sat for a time and shared food with the people of the Sixteenth Kingdom.

Darkness fell, and the champions scurried out of the safety of the Sixteenth Kingdom and into an area of long grasses.

'Well, what shall we do now? It's dark but we can't afford for the Grumblies to see us or they will know we're coming,' said a worried Chippo.

'Pojo, go and talk to those field mice,' Prince Aydo instructed. 'Ask about the tree. Zippo, run on ahead but be careful. We need to know what's ahead of us.'

Pojo did as he was asked and spoke to the field mice, but they too had only heard of the tree so the champions carefully made their way down the middle of the flatlands that led from the Sixteenth Kingdom. They were unaware of evil eyes watching them from the long grass.

Zippo returned, looking puzzled.

'What's wrong, friend?' asked Picco.

'I don't understand,' he said. 'We are so close to the Great Black Divide and the Fifteenth Kingdom, but there are no grumblies to be seen anywhere.'

'We can't trust them,' Leema said. 'We still need to be extra careful otherwise the princess is lost.'

'What was that!' Chippo asked nervously.

'What was what?' Pojo said, looking around wide eyed.

'I thought I heard something over ... '

'Quickly run!' Skudo shouted as the heads of several grumblies appeared out of the long grass. The prince and most of the champions ran to safety at the edge of the nearby forest, but Tracer and Chippo ran straight into a giant sand pit. The Grumblies were hot on the trail of the champions, but luckily failed to see the two stragglers cowering in the sand.

'Oh No!' Skudo said sadly. 'Now we will never surprise the Green Witch.'

Morning came and once again the grumblies went to ground having failed to locate the champions. The prince and eight of the group hid in the forest hoping their friends would soon join them but time was running out.

'Well,' said the prince. 'We must carry on without Tracer and Chippo for it's time to cross the Great Divide.'

They reluctantly left the cover of Willow Wood and edged toward the black pathway, stretching out in front of them like a great black scar across the land. Zippo took the lead and ran as fast as he could. Prince Aydo and the others watched as he reached the other side unscathed.

'Is everyone ready?' the Prince asked.

'Do you think we'll find food on the other side?' Dando asked as his tummy rumbled loudly. The prince frowned at him, then gave the command, 'Let's go!'

The champions ran for all they were worth and were halfway across the divide when the ground began to rumble.

'Oh no!' Picco said.

'What's happening?' cried Laima.

'Don't stop! Run!' the prince shouted. The champions had failed to notice the great metal chariot speeding towards them. The ground rumbled, causing Leema to lose her balance, screaming in pain as she fell to the floor. As quick as a flash Zippo ran and plucked her away from the chariots spinning wheels.

'Thank you, Zippo!'

'All part of the service, Leema,' Zippo smiled.

Once the champions had made their way across the flatlands of the Fifteenth Kingdom they continued until they reached the edge of the Great Wood. By now the sun was shining, birds were singing, and a cool summer breeze swept between the trees. They decided to rest a while and had almost forgotten what they had set out to do. Pojo sat listening to a sparrow as it joyfully greeted the morning air.

'Prince Aydo! Come quickly!' he shouted.

'What is it?' The prince asked.

'That bird. It sings of green leaves, summer berries and a tree called Wizioki.'

'Quickly,' the Prince replied. 'Ask the bird where we can find this tree.' As Pojo turned to speak to the sparrow, it flew from the tree.

'It's getting away!' Pojo shouted as he jumped to his feet. The champions ran excitedly through the wood, trying to follow the bird. Jumping over bushes and piles of leaves, trying not to lose sight of the little sparrow.

'Ouch!' boomed a loud voice. Zippo had tripped and fallen over a large tree root trailing across the forest floor. As he dusted himself off, he looked around to see where the voice had come from.

'Up here you silly little man.' Zippo looked up and found himself staring at the most magnificent oak tree he had ever seen.

'Well, introduce yourself. Who has disturbed my summer snooze?' Zippo was taken aback.

'It is I. Zi, Zip, Zippo. I am one of King Even's Champions.'

'Are you now?' The great tree boomed. 'So what is it that brings you to the sheltered glade of Wizioki?'

Zippo, together with Prince Aydo and the others, sat beneath the tree and told the great oak of their plight. Wizioki looked at the group of tired travellers and frowned.

'Oh my, you are in a mess. We'll have to think very carefully how to proceed.'

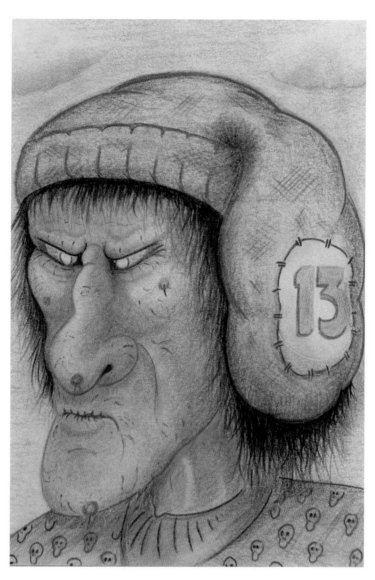

The Green Witch

The Green Witch screamed angrily.

'What do you mean they got away!' The grumblies scattered to all four corners of the room, leaving Grim and Grubb to face the angry witch.

'From now on,' she hissed. 'The two of you will personally ensure those meddling fools get nowhere near the princess.'

'Don't worry, mother,' Grim said as an evil smile came across his face. 'We have guards all around the flatlands, in the long grasses and along the flowing river. Grubb and I will personally guard the princess and no one will get past us.'

'They had better not!' the Green Witch replied menacingly. 'Or you'll be sorry!'

W izioki rustled his leaves and looked

down at the sorry band of champions.

'Well, my friends, with so may Grumblies to get past

there's only one possible way into the witch's stronghold.

You must get as close to the Flowing River as you can

under the cover of darkness. Do not attempt to cross the

bridge - it will be heavily guarded. You will have to use

my magic leaves to float across the river. I will send some

squirrels ahead of you to leave a pile of them by the water's edge.'

'But how are we to enter the Thirteenth Castle?', Prince Aydo asked.

'To the west of the flatlands you will find a rabbit warren. Enter, but be careful as only one of the rabbit tunnels will take you into the castle. From there on it's up to you,' Wizioki said.

The prince and the champions looked grimly at one another. They knew what had to be done. They thanked Wizioki and with time running out they left the Fourteenth Kingdom and continued wearily on their way, avoiding the giants as they continued to pound past, wielding their massive clubs, launching the great white

rocks. By nightfall they could see the river and just bey-
ond, the dreaded Thirteenth Kingdom.

'Grumblies!' said Skudo. 'They're taking up position
across the river!' Quickly the champions ran into a giant
sandpit and carefully made their way to the top to peer
over at the great river.

'Look,' said Skudo. 'Over there. A pile of oak leaves.'

'If we can reach them without being seen, we'll stand a
chance of getting across the river,' Prince Aydo said op-
timistically.

As quiet as mice, the champions made their way into
the pile of leaves that had been carefully placed by the
squirrels. They considered their next move.

'I will go first,' Laima whispered. 'I will be able to tell Leema through my thoughts if it's safe for the rest of you to cross.'

Laima waited until a lone cloud blocked out the light from the moon and pushed an oak leaf into the flowing river. Prince Aydo and the champions watched nervously as she made her way across, finally reaching the other side where she climbed onto the riverbank and covered herself with the wet leaf.

'She made it,' Prince Aydo said. Leema informed the group that Laima had told her it was safe to go across the river. One by one the champions floated across and soon only Dando and Leema were left. As Dando pushed his leaf into the river it became clear to him that one leaf wouldn't be enough to keep him afloat so with three oak leaves beneath him he set off. Suddenly Leema told him to wait.

'Laima has just warned me that grumbly guards are getting close.' It was too late. Dando had by now floated halfway across the river. As he drifted across his thought's, once again, went to his stomach - I hope there's food to eat in the witch's castle. As Dando reached the far bank of the river, he spotted two grumbly guards just above him. He hung onto a root sticking out of the river bank and remained as still as he could for what seemed like an eternity before the guards finally moved on, allowing him to climb the bank and rejoin his friends.

It wasn't long before Leema joined them. Hiding beneath the leaves they crawled past the remaining grumblies and hid amongst the long grasses.

'I'm starving,' Dando whispered. 'I haven't eaten for days.'

'Be quiet, Dando!' the prince whispered back. 'Zippo, use your speed and try to find a way into the castle.' Zippo darted about in the dark and soon returned with good news.

'I've found an entrance, but we need to move quickly while it's unguarded.' The champions left the cover of the long grasses and soon entered a rabbit warren where they stood in amazement at the sight before them. There were so many tunnels to choose from.

'Which way do we go?' Skudo asked.

'Leave it to me,' Pojo said. 'I'll go and talk to the rabbits.' Pojo approached a small group of rabbits and shortly after one agreed to show them to the way to the Thirteenth Castle.

Suddenly, with a loud crash, Dando fell into a heap on the tunnel floor.

'I don't believe it!' Picco said angrily. ' He's fallen asleep!' Loud snoring echoed around the rabbit warren.

'I can't wake him,' Picco said.

'Then we must leave him here,' the prince said. 'We can't afford to wait any longer.' Now they numbered only seven, but bravely they followed the rabbit down the long and twisting route to the castle. Eventually the rabbit stopped by a chink of light shining down from the roof of the tunnel. Picco climbed onto the rabbit's back and realised he was beneath a stone slab that he assumed was part of the floor of the castle. Slowly but surely, Picco moved the stone slab and carefully peered into a dingy passageway.

'All clear,' he whispered. 'Let's go we have no time to lose.'

As the champions made their way through the entrance and into a dimly lit hall the floor beneath them seemed to move.

Within seconds all seven heroes were whipped into the air, trapped in a great net swinging from a high beam. The hall burst into light and riotous laughter echoed all around them.

'Ha Ha Hah!' The Green Witch cackled. 'You fools walked right into my trap. What a surprise you will be for the princess on her wedding day.'

As the hall filled with singing, jeering Grumblies, the prince declared that they had failed. Soon it would be morning and Princess Faithful would be married to Grim. The forlorn champions look down on the wicked Green Witch and her loyal grumblies as they sang and danced into the night.

The prince feared the worst, but one by one the Grumblies fell to the floor and soon even the Green Witch crashed to the ground unconscious.

'What's happening?' Picco asked as once again, laughter echoed around the hall.

'Ho, Ho, Ho! What a sorry sight you all are.'

'Chippo!' The champions cheered. 'It's you!'

'Not just me,' Chippo said. 'Look above you.'

Grim

'Dando!' the prince exclaimed. 'We couldn't wake you!

We thought all was lost.' Dando and Tracer using all of

their strength lowered the bundle to the floor.

'What's happened to the witch and her grumbles?' Laima asked.

'We'll explain later,' Chippo said. 'We don't have much time left to save the princess.' The champions searched the castle, and soon the only place left was a room located at the top of the castle. They made their way up the tower and when they arrived, Tracer peered through the key-hole to find the princess guarded by Grim and Grubb.

'We'll need to move quickly,' the prince whispered. 'Dando. Quickly, go and retrieve the net from the Great Hall?' Dando ran back to find the grumblies were beginning to stir. He gathered up the net as quickly as he could, then returned to the others. One by one they took up their positions, then Picco thumped his fist heavily against the door. Bang! Bang! Bang!

Grim and Grub jumped to their feet and edged toward the door.

'Who's there!' Grubb shouted.

'It's me, you cowards. Picco the Great of the Fourteenth Kingdom.' Grim and Grubb shook with rage and tore open the door.

'Now!' Shouted the prince. Before they realised what was happening, Grim and Grubb were covered by the net and Zippo raced around them in a flash, tying a rope around their feet.

'Ho, Ho,' Picco laughed. 'You look a much better sight than us in that net.'

'My Champions,' Princess Faithful said. 'I never thought I would see you again.'

'We must leave immediately, Princess,' Dando said. 'The grumblies are beginning to wake up.' The princess and the champions ran across the great hall as the grumblies sat rubbing their eyes.

'This way, Princess,' Tracer said as he jumped into the rabbit hole. They quickly made their way through the warren and as they reached the entrance, they heard the Green Witch's screams. She was close behind with the grumblies. The champions left the warren and ran to the Flowing River, only to discover the wind had blown away the leaves they were going to use to escape.

'To the bridge!' Prince Aydo shouted as the Green Witch closed in on them.

'Now we've got them!' she screamed. 'The grumblies at the bridge will hold them up long enough for us to catch up.'

Picco saw the evil creatures heading towards the champions. 'Grumblies!' He shouted but before he could utter another word, the prince, princess and the champions were soaring high into the morning sky, snatched up by a flock of sparrows.

'Who are you, my feathered friends?' asked the princess.

'Wizioki sent us,' one sparrow replied.

'Hooray!' Chippo cheered. 'That's the last we'll see of the Green Witch and her evil Grumblies.'

'Don't be so sure,' Laima said. 'Look behind us.' The Green Witch had summoned a mob of black crows and along with the grumbles they were rapidly catching up with the sparrows.

'Hold on tight!' The sparrow leader tweeted. The champions held tightly to the sparrows legs as they swooped into the forest, but it was too late! The Green Witch was upon them, lunging at the princess, trying to pull her from the small birds grip. Grim and Grub flew in and tried to grab her, but the sparrow held on tightly. Black feathers filled the air, but as they went spinning towards the ground a great white rock tore through the sky.

'Fore!' One of the giants shouted.

'Hooray!' Chippo shouted.

'Get them, you fools,' the Green Witch screamed to the Grumblies flying in on the remaining crows. The chase was still on, but the sparrows were becoming exhausted in their efforts to stay in front of the crows and hold on to the princess and her champions.

Once again they swooped down into the forest and this time managed to reach a sheltered glade, hitting the forest floor with a bump. The sparrows directed their passengers to a hidden entrance where they quickly ran for cover.

'Where are we?' Chippo whispered.

A voice came from within the cave - 'Be quiet!' The champions looked at one another, confused. Where had the voice come from? Outside, the Green Witch and her Grumblies were screaming and cursing, searching the forest floor for what seemed an eternity.

***

Hours passed and eventually the forest returned to silence as the rowdy group headed away from the glade. A squirrel appeared and spoke to Pojo.

'All clear friend.' The princess and the champions breathed a great sigh of relief.

'Now then,' said Chippo. 'Where exactly are we?'

'Why don't you go outside and look for yourselves.' It was the strange voice from within the cave. Feeling puzzled, they made their way out of the cave and back into the forest.

'Wizioki!' Cheered Chippo.

'Yes, my friends,' the wise old tree said. 'You thought you were in a cave, but you were inside of me all the time.'

'It was your voice we were hearing,' laughed Picco.

'It was and I can tell you that the Green Witch was last seen chasing Grim and Grubb back to the Thirteenth Castle.' Wizioki roared with laughter.

'Is anyone else feeling hungry?' Dando asked.

'Sit yourselves down and we will eat,' Wizioki said. 'My woodland friends will bring you something to fill your bellies. The princess and the champions sat down to eat.

'Now then,' Prince Aydo said, looking at Chippo. 'How did you get us out of the net at the Thirteenth Castle?'

'Well,' said Chippo. 'After we managed to climb out of the sandpit, Tracer followed your trail and we crossed the Great Black Divide - eventually we found Wizioki.'

'Yes,' Tracer said. 'Wizioki told us about the leaves by the Flowing River and having got across we made our way to the rabbit warren. Having got inside, we found it too dark to see which tunnel you went down.'

'It was then that we heard the snoring,' Chippo laughed. 'We followed the noise and found Dando asleep at the tunnel entrance.'

'Yes,' the prince said. 'But what happened to the Green Witch and her Grumblies at the castle?'

'That's simple,' answered Chippo. ' You see, it was Dando that gave us the idea. Because he was hungry he had eaten a berry from the bushes in the long grass, and it was that fruit that sent him into a deep sleep. So, I

simply crushed a couple of berries into my hip flask and

poured the juice into the Grumble Punch.'

'Well done!' Cheered the princess. 'From this day on

you will surely be known as the Champions of the Even

Kingdom!'

The End